The Lizard Who Followed Me Home

By Kate Allen

Illustrated by
Jim Harris

The Kumquat Press

Special thanks to

Lauren, Ted, Wilma, James S., Susie, Jeff,
Diane, Marion, Jim, Lorie, Joanne, Kathy,
Karen, Reed, Jim B., and Jenny Sue .

Design and Production by Albion Publishing Group, Santa Barbara, California
FIRST EDITION
FIRST PRINTING, 1995
ISBN 1-887218-01-7
Library of Congress Catalog Number   95-079581
The Lizard Who Followed Me Home by Kate Allen; Illustrations by Jim Harris — 1st edition
32 pages
Summary: An adventure with an unexpected companion

Manufactured in Hong Kong

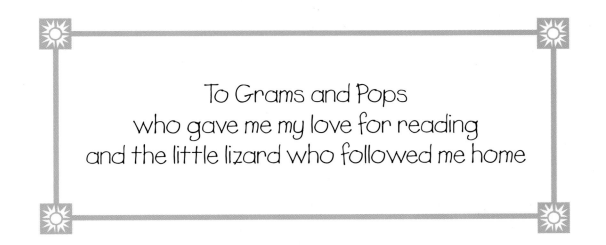

To Grams and Pops
who gave me my love for reading
and the little lizard who followed me home

☀ **It** all started when my family and I were moving to California.

We lived in Kansas. There were boxes stacked everywhere, when my Mom said, " We better go see Grams before we move so far away."

From behind a pile of boxes Dad yelled, "I agree".

And I answered, "Yesssssss!"

That's why, as soon as we finished packing all of our belongings, we flew to Florida to see my Grandmother.

Of course, Grams was delighted to have us visit. Especially me—we love to take long walks on the beach. After one of these walks Grams and I sat down in her yard. Feeling nice and cozy, we took off our shoes and socks and counted our hundreds of shells.

Then I noticed a visitor sitting beside us.

It was a green Florida lizard. Grams tried to shoo it away but it didn't move an inch.

It just sat there and stared.

"Would you look at that," said Grams. "It looks like it wants to say something."

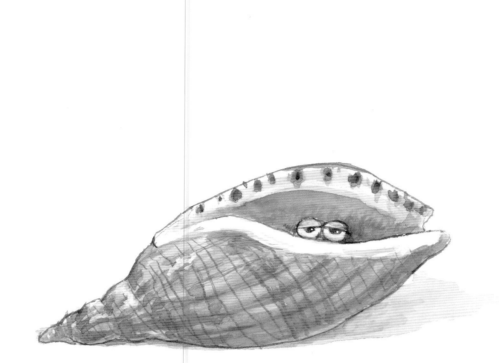

But of course, it couldn't talk, and we gathered up our shells, socks, and shoes and headed for the house.

As we passed the laundry room, Grams suggested we throw our socks into the washing machine.

We started it up and went to lunch.

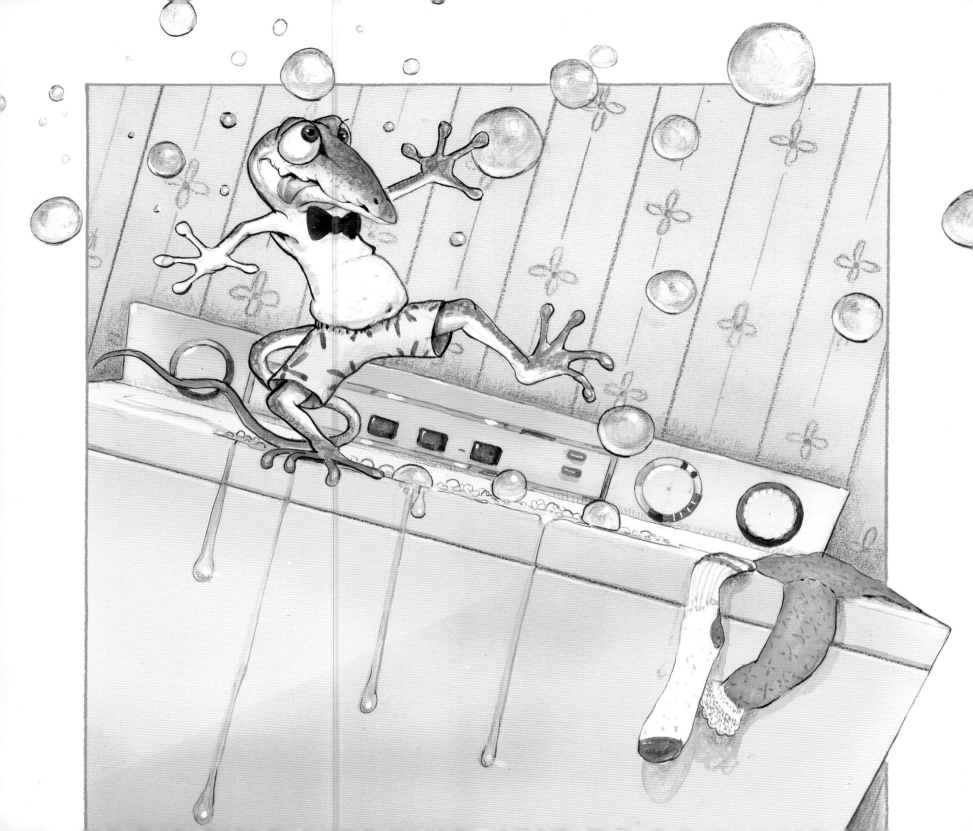

Later that day, I opened the lid of the washing machine and I jumped three feet.

"Whoa— How did you get in there?" I said.

It swayed back and forth for a minute and slowly jumped off.

I finished putting the clothes from the washer into the dryer.

As I walked away, something caught my eye, I turned around and there it was again. That green lizard was stuck on the window inside the dryer, with clothes going around it in every direction.

I quickly stopped the dryer and took the lizard out.

"You silly old lizard—go outside where you belong."

But once again, it just stared at me.

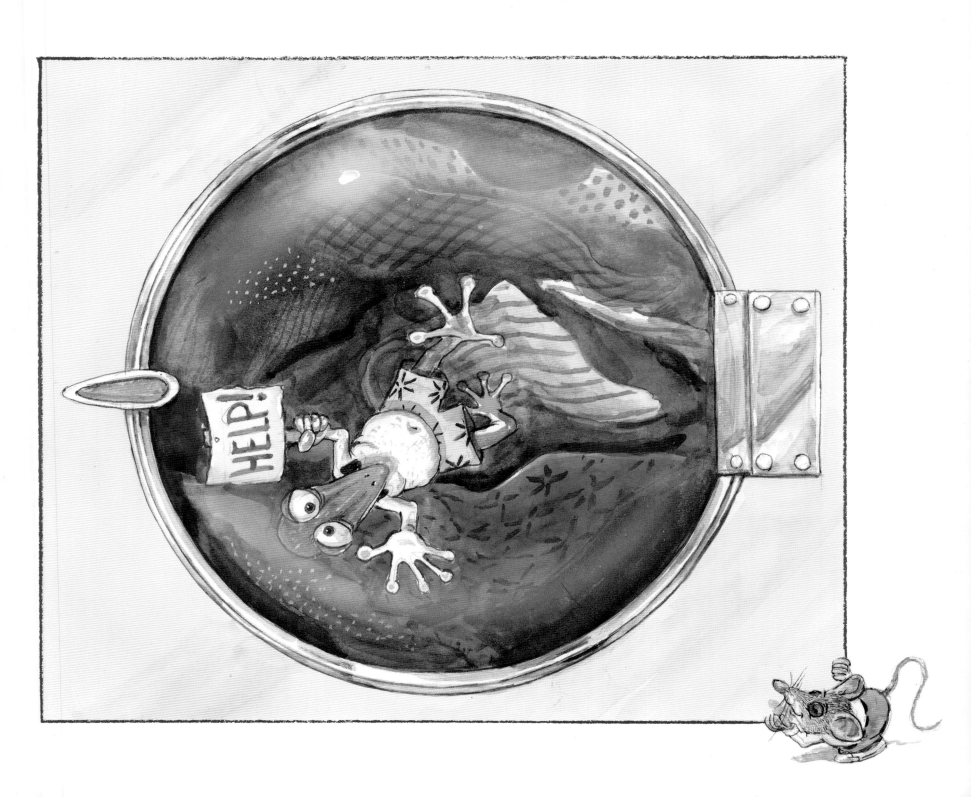

Just then, Grams' dog LuLu rounded the corner of the laundry room and she spotted the lizard.

"No, LuLu, no!" I screamed.

But off they went jumping and leaping, with LuLu barking, trying to catch that silly lizard.

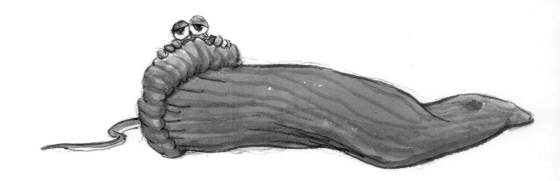

All over the house it went-up the stairs, over Grams' feet, and finally, into a closet.

"Grams!" I yelled. "Come here quickly!"

But neither of us could find the lizard.

LuLu lost interest and stopped sniffing and went to sleep.

When it was time for us to leave, we were all very sad.

Grams baked us delicious chocolate chip cookies, and she cried.

"It's okay Grams, we'll be back soon." I said, with a hug.

Mom asked her to come visit us in California.

Holding onto to LuLu, Grams said good—by and blew kisses until I couldn't see her anymore.

On the plane, traveling back to Kansas, I ate Grams' cookies and thought about what happened to the lizard.

I decided it probably escaped through a window at Grams' house.

When we arrived home, Mom opened her suitcase, and out leaped the green lizard!

She screamed, she jumped, and she cried out, all at the same time!

Dad came running!

I started screaming too!

We chased the lizard through the house over the boxes, and around the furniture. Even with the three of us in pursuit, somehow we lost it.

Mom sat down and said, "I have a headache."

With a face as red as a beet, Dad declared, "Stop this ridiculous search! We're moving anyway."

However, I secretly continued to look for the lizard.

The next day, the moving men loaded everything we owned into the moving vans.

Even with the house empty, I did not find the lizard anywhere.

Dad was anxious and shouted, "Let's get this show on the road!"

So we said good-by to our old house and set out for our new one.

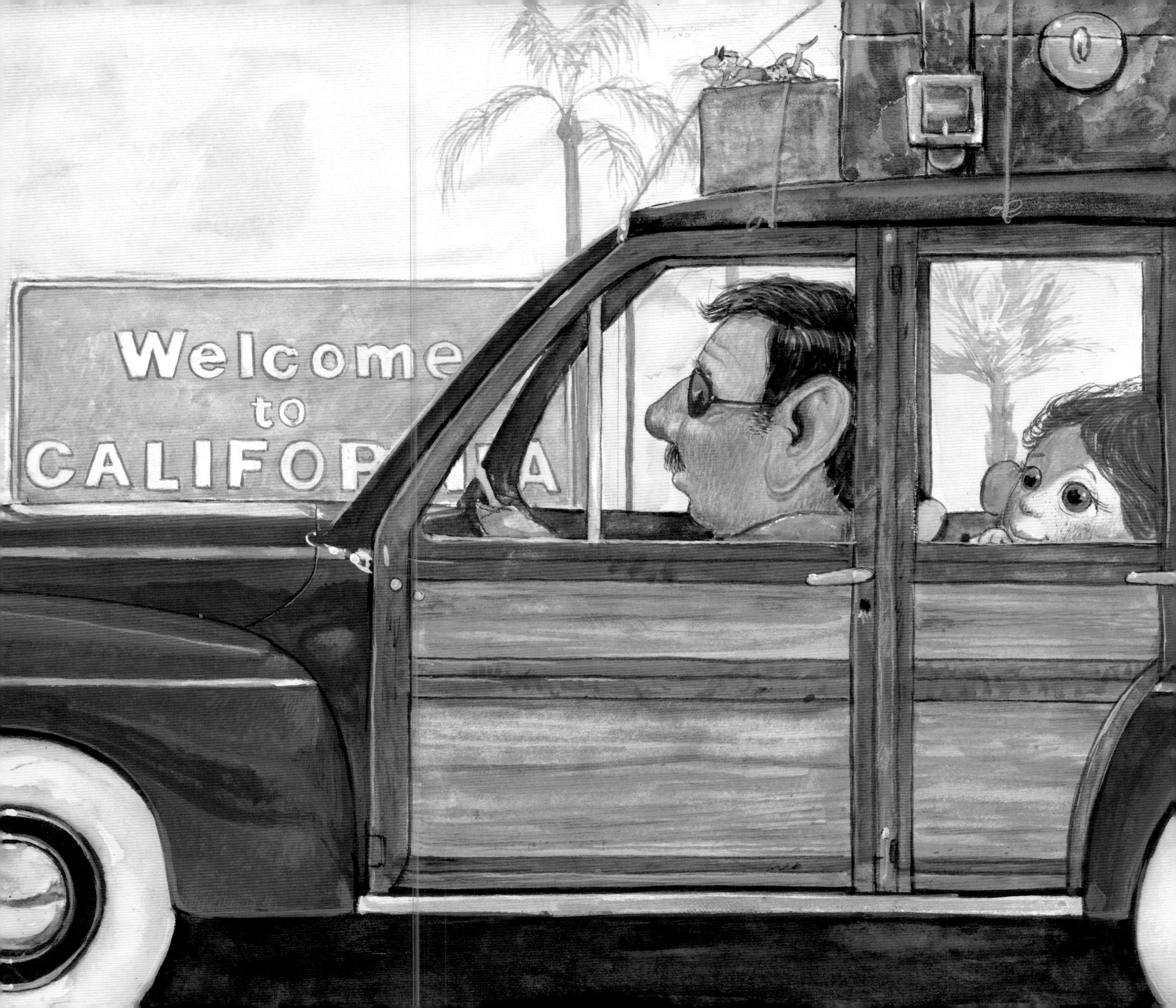
Welcome
to

We arrived in California five days later. Vans, cars, people,
boxes and, of course, one green lizard.
Yes, it hitched a ride to California.
There it was, staring at me once again!

And do you know, it now lives in our garden in California.
It still stares at me like it wants to say something.
And, if I'm very, very quiet, I believe I hear that Florida lizard
telling all of the California lizards how it followed me home.

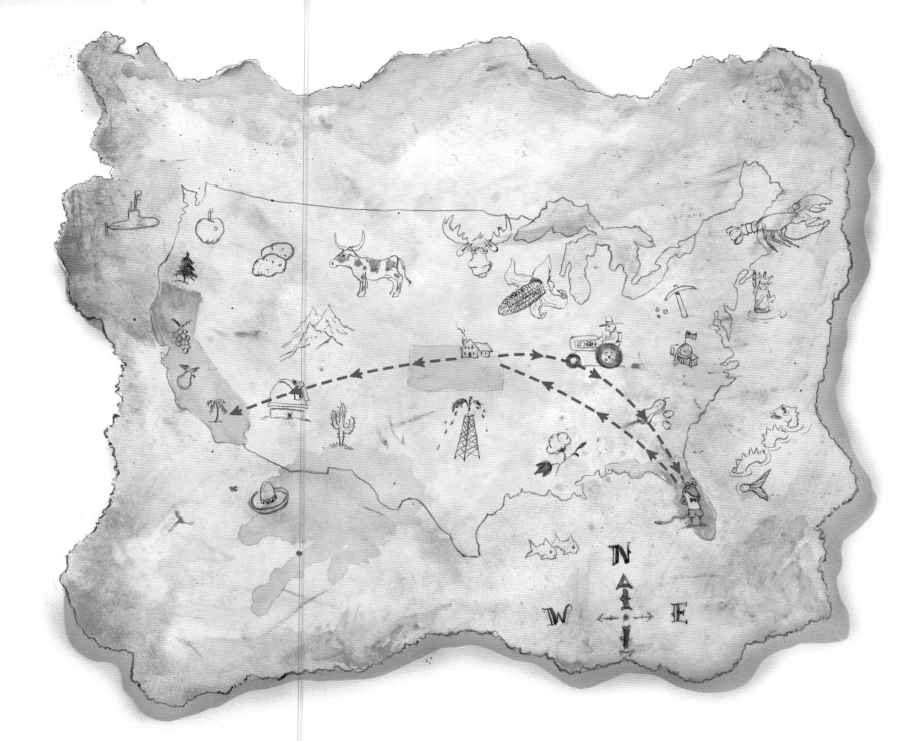

My Journey with One Silly Green Lizard

A LIZARD can be scary at first. It looks strange and moves quickly. Many live in my garden and scamper among my shrubs, trees, and wood piles. I like to make myself comfortable and watch the little acrobats perform. The routines include parachuting, push-ups, head bobbing, and tongue-licking. Exceptionally good listeners, lizards make great friends. One particular lizard loves to tease my dog Ziggy. For hours the two play "find-and-catch". And I am glad Ziggy can find, but never catch. As more and more land is developed the lizard population is diminishing, and few states feel the need to protect the creatures. Besides playing a vital role in our environment, the little reptiles provide richness, discovery, and fun to our own lives. I respect and love all my lizard friends.

Kate

Kate Allen, Author

KATE ALLEN lives on a ranch in Southern California where she raises one husband, one daughter, three horses, seven dogs, eight birds, four chickens, two bunnies, two ducks, one turkey and an iguana named Wimpy. When she can she loves to spend time on an island in Florida with her family and several green lizards. Kate is currently writing a book for women and several other children's books.

Jim Harris, Illustrator

Best known for his humorous illustrations of children's books, Colorado illustrator JIM HARRIS brings to his art experience with clients as diverse as National Geographic Special Publications, The Danbury Mint, and Sesame Street. During his thirteen years as a freelance illustrator, first near Chicago and now in rural Colorado, Jim's illustrations have appeared on greeting cards, posters, magazines, calendars and collectibles as well as children's and young adult titles. Many of Jim's illustrations have won awards, among them the Silver Medal from the Society of Illustrators' Annual Exhibition and the Certificate of Merit from Communication Arts.